Riley's Cake

P. 1A (24)

By Jay Sanders

Illustrated by Nick Bland

Riley looked at the big pink cake in the cook book.

"Look, Gran!" said Riley.

"I want to make this cake today!"

"Mmmmm," said Gran.

"That cake does look good.

Let's get all the things

we need to make it."

Riley and Gran

made the big pink cake.

Grandad came inside for lunch.

"That cake looks good,
and it smells good too!" he smiled.
"Can we eat it?"

"No!" Riley laughed.
"This cake is not for you.
This cake is for
my best friend Sierra.
It is her birthday today,
and I made the cake for her."

After lunch, Riley and Gran
put pink icing on the cake.
Then they put on seven candles.

Riley put the cake
in a big blue box.

"Gran, can we take the cake
to Sierra's house now?" said Riley.

"Yes," said Gran.
"We can walk there."

"Happy Birthday, Sierra!"
Riley smiled.

"I have a surprise for you!"

Sierra looked very happy.

"Thank you," she said.

"Can I open the box now?"

"Yes," said Riley.

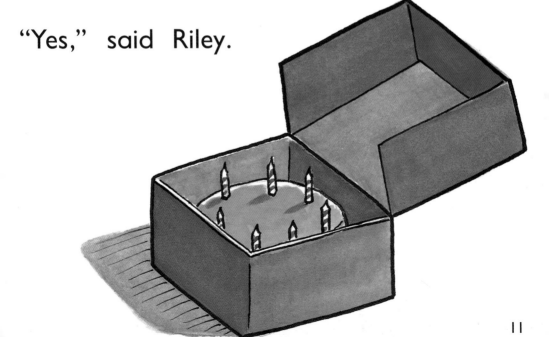

Sierra opened the big blue box.
"Oh thank you, Riley!" she said.
"This cake looks good!"

Sierra's big brother
came out of the house.

"What is inside the box?" he said.

"It is a big pink cake," said Sierra.
"Riley made it for me!"

Sierra's big brother looked at Riley.

"Boys don't make cakes," he said.

"Yes, they do," Riley said.
"I make cakes with my gran
all the time.
I like cooking."

"Riley is the best cook at school,"
said Sierra.
"Come on! Let's go inside
and eat the cake."

"This cake is very good, Riley.
Boys **can** make cakes!"
said Sierra's big brother.

"Yes," Riley laughed. "They can!"